GAUTHIER DAVID is a children's author, illustrator, and singer-songwriter. He has collaborated on several books with his partner Marie Caudry. *Letters from Bear* is their English language debut. Gauthier and Marie live with their children in the Drôme, France, at the edge of a forest where they can sometimes see wolves. Visit his website at gogocosmos.free.fr.

MARIE CAUDRY is a graduate of the Fine Arts School of Bordeaux and has illustrated a number of books. Three days before the birth of their child Arto, Marie began a series of paintings about globe-trotting bears—and these paintings inspired Gauthier to write the story of *Letters from Bear*. Visit Marie's website at mariecaudry.free.fr or follow her on Instagram @mariecaudry.

For our children, Arto and Anna.

First published in the United States in 2020
by Eerdmans Books for Young Readers,
an imprint of Wm. B. Eerdmans Publishing Co.
Grand Rapids, Michigan

www.eerdmans.com/youngreaders

Originally published in Belgium as *Les lettres de l'ourse*
by Gauthier David and Marie Caudry
© Autrement 2012 for the first edition
© Casterman 2017

English language translation © Sarah Ardizzone 2020

Manufactured in China.

29 28 27 26 25 24 23 22 21 20   1 2 3 4 5 6 7 8 9

Library of Congress Cataloging-in-Publication Data

Names: David, Gauthier, 1976- author. | Caudry, Marie, 1978- illustrator. |
   Ardizzone, Sarah, 1970- translator.
Title: Letters from Bear / Gauthier David, Marie Caudry ; translated by
   Sarah Ardizzone.
Other titles: Lettres de l'ourse. English
Description: Grand Rapids, Michigan : Eerdmans Books for Young Readers,
   2020. | Audience: Ages 5-9 | Summary: Bear sends updates on her
   adventures as she travels to visit Bird, who has migrated south for the
   winter.
Identifiers: LCCN 2019030854 | ISBN 9780802855367 (hardcover)
Subjects: CYAC: Bears–Fiction. | Birds–Fiction. | Letters–Fiction.
Classification: LCC PZ7.1.D33595 Le 2020 | DDC [E]–dc23
LC record available at https://lccn.loc.gov/2019030854

The illustrator would like to thank the Centre National du Livre for its support.

MIX
Paper from
responsible sources
FSC® C104723

Letters *from* Bear

GAUTHIER DAVID • MARIE CAUDRY

TRANSLATED BY SARAH ARDIZZONE

Eerdmans Books for Young Readers

Grand Rapids, Michigan

Hello Bird,

Have you arrived safely in the south,
to your island in the sun?
I'm missing you already.
I enjoyed our summer together so much!
Why do you have to migrate every year?

In a week, winter will be here.
All the animals are gathering chestnuts
and acorns inside their caves, nests, and dens.
But I don't have the heart to make my home
ready for hibernation.

I've decided to write to you every day,
so that I can be close to you.
The wind will deliver my letters.

Bye for now, Bird.

Yours,
Bear

Dear Bird,

I've made up my mind.
I'm coming to find you on the other side of the world.
All our friends have wished me a safe journey.
"Don't get too hot," said Badger.
"Bring me back a coconut," said Fox.
"We'll be thinking of you," said Beaver.

They gave me a hazelnut for good luck,
a mossy pillow, and a drawing of the lake.
So you see, I'll be carrying a little bit of each of them with me.
If I feel sad sometimes, these tiny things will comfort me.

Here I come, Bird!

Yours,
Bear

Dear Bird,

I haven't ventured so far from home before.

I'm in the dark forest now, where no one ever goes.

There are huge tracks hollowed out of the ground.

I just fell into one of them.

I hope there aren't any trolls.

I'm glad I'm joining you, but I'm sort of frightened too.

I can't wait to leave this place.

It feels as if I'm being watched.

Kisses and goosebumps,

Bear

Hello Bird,

I was snared in a sailor's fishing net.
Luckily, a mermaid cast a spell on him.
He jumped into the water and loosened his net.
She saved my life!
I'll send her a pot of honey to say thank you.
She's never tasted honey before.
She only eats salty seaweed.

Bye for now,
Your dripping wet Bear

Dear Bird,

I'm writing to you from the top of a volcano.

The earth is the color of night here,

and the stones are scalding hot.

My paws are roasting.

There are strange creatures rising up out of the lava lakes.

Is that what's called a mirage?

I'm enclosing a little sand inside this letter.

Sand that sparkles like the stars.

See you soon, Bird.

Dear Bird,

I'm lost in a cloud of dust.
All around me, I can hear horses neighing
and pounding their hooves.
I've found shelter inside a dead tree.
A stag and an owl are hiding here too.
They tell me there's a war going on.

I think of you, and then I feel safer.

Yours,
Bear

Dear Bird,

Calm has been restored.
The horses are gone and the dust has cleared.
Owl drew a map on the ground and showed me
a route that avoids the battlefields.
The way is longer, but less dangerous.
I'm going to take the path he suggested.

Bye for now, Bird.

Yours,
Bear

Dear Bird,

I hope my silence didn't worry you.
Everything's fine.
I'm eating gooseberry jelly with a friendly cat.
I told him my story, and he invited me to stay at his place.
He lives beneath a pile of branches in a beautiful birch forest.
Tomorrow, I'm planning to rest. I need it.
I haven't slept for nearly two weeks.
I'd like to dream about you.

Be patient, Bird. I'm coming.

Yours,
Bear

Dear Bird,

Today is a big day for the cat and his friends.
Squirrel from the neighboring forest is turning one hundred.
And he's invited me to his birthday celebration!
It's a costume party. I don't know yet what I'm going as.

I'll catch you later, Bird.

Yours,
Bear

Dear Bird,

There's a big crowd here tonight.
There are wolves, lynxes, wild boars, and children.
They're wearing extraordinary costumes
created from leaves, clay, and fallen branches.
I made a kingfisher mask out of clay.
It's almost as if you were here.

Until tomorrow, my dear Bird.

Yours,
Bear

Hello Bird,

I'm the first one up.
I found a carpet of strawberries and vines
close to the hole where I dozed off.
I'm going to make breakfast for all the guests who are still asleep.
I wish I could share all these experiences with you.

I miss you.

Yours,
Bear

Hello Bird,

I said goodbye to the cat and his friends this morning.
I'm traveling with another bear who is
heading back to her mountains.
She knows all the shortcuts, as well as all the best places
for us to fish for salmon and to sleep.
She's terrific. I bet you'd like her.
The walls of the cave where we're spending the night
are covered with drawings.
You can spot men hunting big animals.
We even found a bear carved into the rock.
It's like a puzzle.
Is this a hermit's cave? Will he surprise us?
We'll soon find out.
I don't feel as frightened now that there are two of us.

I'm getting closer, Bird.

Yours,
Bear

Hello Bird,

I'm on my own again.
I'm making my way with a little sadness in my heart
after saying goodbye to my new friend this morning.
We got along so well together! I even shed a tear or two.

I told her about our country.
She promised me she would come and visit us in the spring.
She really wants to meet you.

I'm so excited at the idea of being near you.
It fills me with courage.

Your Bear isn't very far away now!

Dear Bird,

I'm in the desert.

It's very hot here. So this is the south?

I forgot to fill up my gourd with water before setting off.

Soon I won't have a drop left to drink.

I picture our waterfall, and that makes me feel cooler.

See you very soon,

Your Bear with a parched throat

Dear Bird,

I still have to cross the sea.
I've hollowed out a tree trunk to use as a boat,
but the currents are too strong for me to set out tonight.
I'm feeling happy, so happy.
Tomorrow, I'll be with you.

Yours,
Bear

Hello Bird,

I'm here! Where are you?
I'm waiting for you by the eagle-shaped rock.
Come quickly!

Yours,
Bear

Hello Bird,

How disappointing!
I've traveled the world to find you,
but you're no longer here.
The birds explained everything to me.
You didn't want us to be separated by winter
any more than I did.
So you headed back north to find me.
Which means you didn't receive a single one of my letters!
I've gathered them all up.
I'm taking great care of them
and I'll give them to you on my return.
But I'm still going to write to you every day,
to record the final part of my adventure.

See you soon, my dear Bird.

Yours,
Bear

Dear Bird,

I hope you're not too cold in my den,
and that Fox, Beaver, and Badger
are looking after you.
I'm enjoying discovering the island
you told me so much about:
I've been drinking coconut milk,
swimming with schools of colorful fish,
and listening to the music
from all sorts of different birds.

We're leaving in a few weeks.
I still don't know how.
But your friends have a plan
to get me back to my country.

I'm coming.

Yours,
Bear

Hello Bird,

What a surprise! The birds have built a nest
to fit me so we can migrate together.
They're going to carry me inside it.
I warned them I'm very heavy
and they'll have a hard time lifting me.
That annoyed them, so I'm keeping quiet from now on.

It's a very comfortable nest. I slept in it last night.
I dreamed I was a bird.
I had feathers and wings and I was flying with you.
Badger, Fox, and Beaver were also in my dream.
They were waving at us from down below.
I was so light, when really I weigh hundreds of pounds.

Tomorrow we leave.
Big hugs.

Yours,
Bear

Dear Bird,

Yesterday, we left the island.
I'm flying over the desert, the forests, and the seas
that I crossed by paw.
The air currents are so fast!
I'm writing to you from a cloud where we've made a stop.
I'm glad I've experienced all these adventures.
They've brought me closer to you.
Now I know what it's like when the salty air sticks to your skin.
And you must have experienced the joys
of skating on the frozen lake.
Now we'll understand each other when we talk about winter.

I love you, Bird.
Your Bear